VAMPLETS

WRITTEN BY

GAYLE MIDDLETON
&
DAVE DWONCH

ART BY

AMANDA CORONADO
WITH
BILL BLANKENSHIP

BRYAN SEATON- PUBLISHER
KEVIN FREEMAN- PRESIDENT
SHAWN PRYOR- VP DIGITAL MEDIA
SHAWN GABBORIN- EDITOR IN CHIEF
DAVE DWONCH- CREATIVE DIRECTOR
JASON MARTIN- EDITOR
CHAD CICCONI- CRIES VAMPYRE TEARS
COLLEEN BOYD- ASSOCIATE EDITOR

CHAPTER 1

"A MEETING WITH DESTINY"

WRITTEN BY GAYLE MIDDLETON AND DAVE DWONCH
DRAWN BY AMANDA CORONADO
COLORED BY BILL BLANKENSHIP
LETTERED BY DAVE DWONCH

WHY DID YOU EVER SIGN US UP FOR ZOMBIE GUINEA PIG NEIGHBOR-HOOD WATCH?
SO WE COULD BE TOGETHER MORE OFTEN.
WELL, THE POISON BLACK MUSHROOM TARTS THEY SERVE **ARE** TO DIE FOR.
I LO...
NO!
DON'T SAY IT! YOU KNOW THE CONSEQUENCES!

I CAN'T HELP IT. I LOVE YOU.
DON'T!

POOF
OH, NO...
...A VAMPYRE BABY!
EEEE
"I DON'T KNOW HOW OR WHY THIS IS HAPPENING, BUT IT HAS TO ***STOP!***"

SPONTANEOUS VAMPYRE BIRTHS ARE ON THE RISE--
AND THE VAMPYRES CAN'T BE BOTHERED WITH THE 777 YEARS IT TAKES TO RAISE A VAMPLET.
AND THE WEREWOLVES AND ZOMBIES AREN'T MUCH BETTER!
KEEP OUT!
I CAN APPRECIATE YOUR CONCERN, MR. G, SIR, BUT AFTER WHAT HAPPENED TO THE LAST ONE, WELL...
...THE NIGHTMARE NURSERY NEEDS A NEW GOVERNESS.
NO ONE IN GLOOMVANIA WANTS TO BE IN THE SAME ROOM AS THESE LITTLE MONSTERS, MUCH LESS LOOK AFTER THEM!
AS HEAD OF THE DEPARTMENT OF DEPORTRANSMUTATION, IT'S MY JOB TO FIX PROBLEMS!
PERHAPS IT'S TIME TO... OUTSOURCE?
I KNOW... I KNOW! SEND FOR CYRIL!
SIGH YES, SIR.

SIGH.
YOU ASKED TO SEE ME, MR. G?
YES, CYRIL... I'M SENDING YOU ON A SECRET MISSION.
I NEED YOU TO FIND SOMEONE TO RUN THE NURSERY, AND I'M SENDING YOU TO *THE OUTWORLD* TO DO IT.
I NEED YOU TO FLY FAST, CYRIL. DO IT FOR THE BABIES...*NO!* DO IT FOR *ME!!!*
YES, SIR.
"DID YOU EVER THINK YOU WERE DESTINED FOR GREATNESS?"

YOU CAN
TIPS FOR SUCCESS
CAREER DAY
I MEAN BEFORE YOU BECAME A GUIDANCE COUNSELOR?
LIKE, MAYBE YOU WANTED TO BE A FIREMAN...REALLY SAVE LIVES.
YOU CAN
DO IT!
I DO SAVE LIVES, DESTINY HARPER.
HERE'S THE THING, I HAVE NO IDEA WHAT I WANT TO DO WITH MY LIFE.
I DON'T HAVE ANY SKILLS, I HAVE NO PROSPECTS, NO FRIENDS...
IT SAYS HERE THAT YOU'RE A SOLID 3.0 STUDENT.
CERTAINLY YOU HAVE SOME SKILLS, DESTINY.
I'M GOOD WITH KIDS. WELL, MY SISTER'S KID. IS BABYSITTING A SKILL?
FOR TEN DOLLARS AN HOUR, IT'S A START.

LATER THAT DAY, AFTER SCHOOL, IN THE MALL.
IF I WAS MAKING $10 AN HOUR BABY-SITTING I WOULDN'T BE STUCK AT THIS POINTLESS JOB. UGH.
WOULDN'T BE SO TERRIBLE IF IT WEREN'T FOR THE DUMB HAT.
DESTINY
TOTALLY. MY PARENTS, LIKE, TOTALLY SET IT UP.
I AM SO JEALOUS, BECKS.
I KNOW, RIGHT?
YUM'S
DOGSICL
SO I'LL BE STAYING IN PARIS, RIGHT ON THE CHAMPS-ELYSEES FOR, LIKE, THE WHOLE SUMMER...
...AND ALL I HAVE TO DO IS LOOK AFTER A COUPLE OF SPOILED BRATS!
I SO HATE YOU, BECKS.
I SO HATE YOU, TOO, BECKS.
DESTINY

NOTHING EVER HAPPENS TO ME.
SCHOOL. WORK. REPEAT.
IT'S LIKE THE PERFECT RECIPE FOR BORING.
SIGH...
THANKFULLY, THERE'S THE K AND P.
KNIGHT PAWN
I HIT ALL THE THRIFT STORES AND SHOPS AROUND TOWN, BUT KNIGHT AND PAWN IS THE BEST.
IT'S FILLED WITH ANTIQUES, MUSTY HATS, CLOTHES, KNICK KNACKS AND AN ASSORTMENT OF BIZARRE ODDITIES--
--STUFF THAT NO OTHER PAWN SHOP WOULD TAKE.
HELLO, DESTINY!
HEY, MRS. BLACKTHORNE.

HOW MANY TIMES DO I HAVE TO TELL YOU, GIRL, CALL ME ANNIE.
YES, MRS. BLACKTHORNE. ANY NEW ARRIVALS?
I SPEND HOURS IN THIS OLD PLACE. I LOVE IT HERE.
NOT MUCH, I'M AFRAID. A FEW NEW PIECES, NOTHING SPECIAL.
THERE ARE ALWAYS TREASURES TO BE FOUND.
THIS IS THE ONLY PLACE I FEEL FREE.
WELCOME
THIS PLACE IS AMAZING!

AND THAT'S WHEN I SEE IT.
"SEE" IS THE WRONG WORD.
MORE LIKE IT *CALLS* TO ME.
AS IF IT KNOWS THAT IT'S SUPPOSED TO BE MINE.
YOU ARE SUPPOSED TO BE MINE, AREN'T YOU?
HOW MUCH FOR THE LOCKET, ANNIE?

SCORE!
THAT GIRL.
THERE IS SOMETHING ABOUT HER.
FOR SOME UNEXPLAINABLE REASON I FEEL COMPELLED TO REVEAL MYSELF TO HER.
I AM DRAWN TO HER...

...LIKE A MOTH TO A FLAME.
AND I MUST KNOW WHY.

I... I...
THIS HAS TO BE A DREAM.
AN AMULET OF GLOOMVANIA. THAT IS WHY I WAS DRAWN TO YOU.
BUT THERE'S NO WAY MY MIND CREATED **HIM**.

IT'S... POWER... IS...

...HYPNOTIZING...
I HAVE TO KNOW...

...IS HE REAL?
...IMMEASURABLE...

AH!
YOU SEEK TO DO CYRIL HARM!
TO LURE HIM IN! KILL HIM!
HARPY!
SIREN!
WELL, THAT WAS WEIRD.
MAYBE I ATE TOO MANY CORN DOGS?

AND THE NIGHT JUST KEEPS GETTING WEIRDER.

Looking for adventure?
Thrills? Danger?
Seeking employment in child care services?
Look no further!
The Nightcare Nursery wants YOU!
No experience necessary, inquire at
3370 Graves End Road.
This Sunday ONLY.

TAKING CARE OF BABIES AT NIGHT...*THAT* I CAN DO.
THANK YOU, WEIRD FLYING MOTH MAN!

SUNDAY.
3370 GRAVES END ROAD.
THIS ISN'T OMINOUS OR ANYTHING.
HELLO, OUR FIRST VICTI... GUEST. PLEASE, DO COME IN, GIRL.
H-HELLO. MY NAME IS DESTINY.
AND WHY WOULDN'T IT BE?
PLEASE, DESTINY, COME IN OUT OF THE COLD.
I'VE PREPARED COOKIES AND TEA IN THE DINING ROOM.

PLEASE MAKE YOURSELF COMFORTABLE.
SOMEONE WILL BE BY TO... INTERVIEW YOU SOON.
SLAM!
WELL, IF SOMEONE IS GOING TO AXE MURDER ME, NOW WOULD BE THE TIME.
MAYBE ANSWERING AN AD LEFT BEHIND BY A TALKING MOTH WASN'T SUCH A GOOD IDEA.

UGH! GROSS!

I... I...

ZZZZZZZZ

STOP! STOP!
HAHA HAHA
HAHA
HAHA

OMG! THAT WAS TOO STRANGE!
THUD
OH, THE HORROR!
RASKET SAW EVERYTHING. EVERYTHING! HOW HIDEOUSLY TERRIBLE FOR YOU!
I DON'T KNOW, IT WASN'T SO BAD. HIGHSCHOOL... NOW THAT IS--
--TERRIFYING.
AAIIEEEEEEEEEEE
AAAIIEEEEEE

WAIT... WERE YOU JUST... SCREAMING?
IT SEEMED LIKE THE PROPER THING TO DO, AFTER WHAT YOU'VE JUST BEEN THROUGH.
I SAW IT ALL... THE PURPLE BUNNIES... THE PINK KITTENS... HORRIBLE!
TO HAVE SURVIVED SUCH TORTURE... UNIMAGINABLE!
AFTER THE WEEK I'VE HAD, THE BUNNIES AND KITTENS WERE KIND OF... SWEET.
EXACTLY!
HERE IN GLOOMVANIA, SWEET IS HIDEOUS, AND HIDEOUS IS SWEET!
GLOOMVANIA? NOW I KNOW I MUST BE DREAMING.

WINGS & THINGS
REST ASSURED YOUNG LADY, THIS IS NOT A DREAM.
RASKET THE STINKLESS STINKBUG, AT YOUR SERVICE.
BONES : CLU
SKEL TONS
WELCOME TO GLOOMVANIA.

BUGS ON A STICK!
BUGS ON A STICK
BUGS ON A STICK

"THE TROUBLE WITH NANNIES"

WRITTEN BY GAYLE MIDDLETON AND DAVE DWONCH
DRAWN BY AMANDA CORONADO
COLORED BY BILL BLANKENSHIP & DAVE DWONCH
LETTERED BY DAVE DWONCH

WINGS & THINGS
SKELETONS ON
YOU... KNOW WHO I AM?
INDEED! WELCOME TO GLOOMVANIA, DESTINY HARPER.
OF COURSE! MADAME SIMONE HAS BEEN TALKING ABOUT YOU FOR DAYS!
SHE LIVES TO GOSSIP, AND WHEN WORD GOT OUT THAT A HUMAN WAS GOING TO HELP WITH OUR PREDICAMENT...
PUH... PREDICAMENT?
YOU... YOU DON'T KNOW?
YOU ARE HERE TO SERVE AS THE GOVERNESS AT THE NIGHTMARE NURSERY, AND NO ONE HAS PREPARED YOU?
MADNESS!
A- ALL I DID WAS DRINK SOME BAD TEA. THIS CAN'T BE REAL. YUH- YOU CAN'T BE REAL.

BONES
SKELETONS ONLY
I AM AS REAL AS THE WORLD AROUND YOU, DESTINY HARPER.
WE MUST GET YOU OFF THE STREETS.
IT IS NOT WISE FOR A MORTAL TO WANDER THE STREETS IN THIS PART OF GLOOMVANIA.
SKELETONS ONLY
OH MY GOSH!
GOOD EVENING, LOVELY.

BONES : CLUB
WHAT IS THIS PLACE?
THE BONE'S CLUB.
A PRIVATE CLUB FOR GENTLEMEN SKELETONS ONLY.
DO NOT BE AFRAID, DESTINY HARPER. YOU ARE SAFE, EVEN IN MY UNWORTHY ARMS.
UNWORTHY? WHAT DO YOU MEAN?
RASKET IS THE LOWEST OF THE LOW. A STINKBUG WITH NO STINK!

I AM COMPLETELY USELESS.
NOT STINKING? THAT DOESN'T SOUND *BAD.*
EXACTLY.
AS I SAID BEFORE, DESTINY HARPER, IN GLOOMVANIA SWEET IS HIDEOUS AND HIDEOUS IS SWEET.
RASKET IS AN OUTCAST, FORCED TO CLEAN UP AFTER SKELETONS. THEY HAVE NO SENSE OF SMELL SO NONE ARE OFFENDED BY MY ***STINKLESSNESS!***
WE HAVE SOMETHING IN COMMON.
ON MY WORLD I'M AN OUTCAST TOO.

PERHAPS WE CAN HELP EACH OTHER THEN?
MAYBE.
AGREED!
NO ONE KNOWS HOW OR WHY, BUT VAMPYRE BABIES HAVE BEEN APPEARING... SEEMINGLY FROM THIN AIR FOR YEARS!
AT DAY BREAK WE WILL VISIT THE NIGHTMARE NURSERY, AND SETTLE THIS.
WILL I BE ABLE TO GET HOME?
PERHAPS, BUT FOR NOW REST. THERE IS A COT IN THE STORAGE ROOM. YOU WILL BE SAFE WITHIN.
I WILL PROTECT YOU.
THERE ARE FAR WORSE THAN RASKET CREEPING GLOOMVANIA THIS NIGHT!

THE NEXT DAY.
YOU'RE SURE THIS IS THE PLACE?
ASSUREDLY SO, DESTINY HARPER.
HELLO, MORTAL GIRL. ARE YOU READY TO FULFILL YOUR CONTRACT?
CONTRACT?
AW, PRICEFORTH IS JUST HAVING A LAUGH. I'M MR. G., YOUR NEW BOSS.
COME IN, MS. HARPER!
RASKET?
YOU WILL BE FINE, DESTINY. I WILL BE WITH YOU.
NOT YOU, RASKET.
YOU'VE DONE GOOD WORK, COMMENDABLE EVEN, BUT YOUR PART'S DONE.
I HOPE YOU WILL BE FINE, DESTINY HARPER.

I SEE THE VAMPYRE TEARS DID THEIR JOB.
VAMPYRE TEARS?
IN THE TEA. IT'S HOW TO TRAVEL BETWEEN WORLDS, BUT NEVER YOU MIND.
IT'S TIME TO MEET THE BRATS... AHEM...I MEAN THE BABIES.
THIS-- THIS ISN'T RIGHT! YOU KIDNAPPED ME!
YOU HAVE TO SEND ME BAC-
OOF!
GAH! WHAT THE HECK?
SEE? THEY ALREADY LIKE YOU!
NO WAY AM I TAKING CARE OF THESE...THESE... CREEPY LITTLE THINGS!
SEEMS TO ME THAT YOU DON'T HAVE A CHOICE, NOT IF YOU WANT TO GO HOME.

WHAT DO YOU MEAN?
FREE WILL, DESTINY. *YOU* ANSWERED THE AD. *YOU* DRANK THE TEA.
YOU WANTED THIS.
GET TO KNOW YOUR WARDS WELL, HARPER. TREAT THEM RIGHT-
-DO YOUR JOB-
-AND THEN WE CAN TALK ABOUT GETTING YOU BACK TO BORING OLD EARTH.
BUT... BUT...
...THERE'S MORE OF THEM?
THIS... HOW BAD CAN THIS BE? THEY'RE JUST BABIES, RIGHT?
CHOMP
DESTINY HARPER!

DESTINY!

LET ME IN, DESTINY. QUICKLY!
RASKET! HURRY!

BACK AWAY, VAMPLETS, OR FACE THE WRATH OF A FULLY GROWN STINKBUG!

AHAHHAHA AHAHAHAHAHA
THEY KNOW ABOUT YOUR CONDITION, TOO?
IF YOU'VE EVER SMELLED A STINKBUG, YOU'D KNOW THE DIFFERENCE. REGARDLESS... OFF TO BED, ALL OF YOU!

WHO LET HIM IN?
I DID. AND HIS NAME IS RASKET.
WELL, DON'T LET MR. G. CATCH HIM ON THE GROUNDS. HE'S NOT WELCOME.
HE'S MY FRIEND, AND HE STAYS.
SO BE IT.
LET ME GUESS YOU'RE LILY ROSE.
LILY ROSE
I'D BET THIS IS HOWLISS.
HOWLISS
OH, SO VERY PERCEPTIVE.
CADAVERSON NIGHTSHADE IS OUR TERRIBLE GENIUS. HE LIVES TO CREATE NEW WAYS TO FRIGHTEN OTHERS...
YOU WILL HAVE TO WATCH OUT FOR EVILYN NOCTURNA. HER PSYCHIC POWERS MAKE HER QUITE FORMIDABLE...
BURTON CREEPSON JR. ... HIS ARTISTIC SIDE LEADS TO MANY, MANY RUINED WALLS...
COUNT VLAD VON GLOOM COMES FROM THE DIRECT LINEAGE OF COUNT DRACULA HIMSELF...
...MIDNIGHT MORI IS OUR LATEST ADDITION, SHE APPEARS TO BE A WEAPONS EXPERT.

YOU WILL GET TO KNOW THE REST IN THE COMING MONTHS...
MONTHS?!
...IF YOU SURVIVE.
SURVIVE?!
INDEED. WHILE THE ADULT VAMPYRES ARE LOATHE TO RAISE THEIR CHILDREN THEMSELVES, THEY HAVE A VESTED INTEREST IN HOW YOU FARE IN THE PROCESS.
AND THE OTHER CREATURES... THEIR PARENTS WILL BE JUST AS MINDFUL, AND EVEN LESS PATIENT WITH YOUR PROGRESS!
THEN... THEN I'D BETTER CLEAN THIS PLACE UP!
NO... NO! HOW MANY TIMES MUST RASKET REPEAT HIMSELF? UGLY IS THE PRETTY IN GLOOMVANIA, DESTINY HARPER.
THE BITEMARES MUST INFLICT THE DREAD DREAMS!
THE DUSTMITES MUST THRIVE!
THE STINKBUG IS CORRECT, SAVE FOR ONE DETAIL.
THE BABIES MUST LOOK PERFECTLY PERFECT, MS. HARPER.
THOUGH THEY WANT NOTHING TO DO WITH THEM, THE VAMPYRES DEMAND THEIR BABIES BE FASHION FORWARD.
AND THERE WILL BE MANY EYES ON YOU...TONIGHT IN FACT. YOU AND THE VAMPLETS WILL BE ON DISPLAY AT THE BIZARRE BAZAAR IN JUST A FEW HOURS.

"YOU HAD BEST IMPRESS, GIRL. THE GLOOMVANIANS ARE NONE TOO HAPPY WITH A MORTAL TAKING CARE OF THEIR BABIES."
I'M... I'M AFRAID, RASKET.
BE STRONG, DESTINY HARPER. SHOW NO FEAR,
OPEN
THANKS FOR BEING HERE FOR ME, RASKET.
I KNOW THIS CAN'T BE EASY FOR YOU.

DIDN'T YOU HEAR? I'M THE HERO IN THIS STORY.
FOR A FIGMENT OF MY IMAGINATION, YOU'RE... OKAY.
YOU ARE VERY STRANGE, MORTAL.
SO WHAT DO YOU THINK? SHOULD WE STOCK UP ON BOTTLE BLOOD AND TOYS WHILE WE'RE HERE?
WHAT COULD BE THE HARM IN THAT?
HELLO...ERR... SIR? WOULD YOU HAPPEN TO HAVE ANYTHING FOR VAMPLETS?
Zang-DUN Fraq!
PERHAPS A TRANSLATOR WOULD HELP?
SHRUNKEN HEAD TRANSLATORS
SHRUNKEN HEADS... YOU'RE KIDDING, RIGHT?
SHRUNKEN HEADS

THAT ONE... PENELOPE RANCID. WELL, I GUESS THINGS COULD BE WORSE.
PENELOPE RANCID
IT'LL BE NICE TO HAVE A GIRLFRIEND, NO OFFENSE, RASKET.
WAIT, WHAT?! MY MASTER'S DEGREE IN TRANSLATION GUARANTEES I'LL BE PAIRED WITH A VAMPYRE...
...A YETI AT THE VERY LEAST!
NO WAY AM I GOING HOME WITH A TEENAGED MORTAL!
YOU SOUND LIKE... LIKE A SNOB.
CALL ME WHAT YOU WILL, BUT I'D NEVER HANG WITH SOMEONE LIKE YOU...
...ESPECIALLY IF I HAD, Y'KNOW, LEGS.
AND I THOUGHT YOUR LOOKS WERE GROSS!
YOUR ATTITUDE STINKS!
ADS
YOU WANT TO KNOW WHAT STINKS?
BEING ATTACHED TO A MORTAL.
YOU'RE LUCKY I HAVE STUDENT LOANS TO PAY, 'CAUSE THIS IS GROSS!
WHATEVER. LET'S GO SHOPPING.

AND SOON...
IT SAYS IT'LL BE FOUR FINGERNAILS.
TELL IT WE'LL TAKE THEM!
THIS'LL MAKE A GREAT SCRATCHING POST FOR HOWLISS!
WOW. ARE YOU SURE WE CAN AFFORD IT?
I DON'T SEE HOW YOU CAN AFFORD **NOT** TO GET IT.
BLOOD BOTTLE WARMER
WITH THAT CAULDRON YOU COULD HEAT ALL THE BLOOD IN GLOOMVANIA!
THE KIDS COULD DRINK FOR, LIKE, EVER!
Fresh Brains
REALLY, PENNY?
ZOMBIE BABIES GOTTA EAT, TOO. LOOK AT THOSE EYES. THEY'LL LOVE IT!

YOU KNOW THAT WAS ACTUALLY KIND OF FUN... RIGHT?
MAYBE FOR YOU, LOSER.
OH, YOU KNOW YOU HAD FUN.
I'LL NEVER TELL.
WHAT IS IT, DESTINY HARPER?
WELL, NOW THAT THAT'S SETTLED LET'S GO HOM- OH, NO!
HOWLISS JAILBROKE THE STROLLER PRISON!
I'M DOOMED!

HE IS ONE WEREWOLF BABY. HOW DESTRUCTIVE COULD HE BE-
OH, **NO.**
YOU HAD TO ASK.
WHO CARES! WHEN'S DINNER? I'M FAMISHED.

WHAT DO I DO, RASKET?
CHOMP

IF I WERE YOU, I'D GET OUT OF TOWN AS FAST AS POSSIBLE.

PLEASE LET ME BY. I HAVE TO-

ooOFF!!

THIS IS THE ONE, THE HUMAN THAT CAUSED ALL THIS TROUBLE.
I SAY WE FEED HER TO THE ZOMBIES AND GET IT OVER WITH.
DOESN'T SEEM LIKE YOU'D NEED A TRANSLATOR FOR THIS ONE. YOU'RE *TOAST!*
TO BE CONTINUED!

LEGEND OF THE GHOST PONY

CONVENTION EXCLUSIVE COVER

PRICEFORTH

VAMPLETS #1 VARIANT COVER

A MEETING WITH DESTINY
ORIGINAL GRAPHIC NOVEL ADVERTISEMENT